The Sun and the Wind

Illustrated by Francesca di Chiara

Retold by Mairi Mackinnon

Based on a story by Aesop

It was a fine summer's day.
The sun shone down. He was pleased
to see everyone enjoying themselves.

"Look at me!"
he said, proudly.

"Huh," said the wind, grumpily. "Listen to me."

He blew a sudden squall, whipping up the waves, snatching sunhats and upending umbrellas.

"See how strong I am," said the sun, melting an ice cream.

"Oh, but I'm stronger," howled the wind, blowing dark stormclouds across the sky.

"You? Stronger than me? Prove it!" said the sun.

"See that man? I bet you can't take his coat off."

"I bet I CAN," said the wind and, puffing out his cheeks, he blew as hard as he could.

The birds turned somersaults in the air...

...and the man nearly fell over backwards.

"Blow, wind, blow," teased the sun. "Look, he's cold. He's buttoning his coat."

The wind blew harder.

The man put up his hood, and pulled his coat tighter.

The wind blew his hardest, and the man hurried into a shelter. "I give up," groaned the wind.

"My turn," said the sun.
The wind was still.
The man looked out.

The sun shone with all his might,
and the birds started singing again.

The man pulled back his hood.
"He's warm now," said the sun.

Hotter and hotter the sun shone.

The man smiled, and unbuttoned his coat.

When he reached the beach,
he took it off altogether.

"I win!" crowed the sun.

The man took off his shoes, and his socks too.
He sat on the sand with a blueberry ice cream.

And the wind went off in a huff.

Edited by Jenny Tyler and Lesley Sims

Designed by Caroline Spatz

Digital manipulation by John Russell

This edition first published in 2014 by Usborne Publishing Ltd, 83-85 Saffron Hill, London EC1N 8RT, England.
www.usborne.com Copyright © 2014, 2008 Usborne Publishing Ltd. The name Usborne and the devices 🎈 🌐 are Trade Marks
of Usborne Publishing Ltd. All rights reserved. No part of this publication may be reproduced, stored in a retrieval system,
or transmitted in any form or by any means, electronic, mechanical, photocopying, recording or otherwise,
without the prior permission of the publisher. UE.